FOR

TOMMIE AND
KATHLEEN

COME ON-ALONG, FISH!

COME ON-ALONG, FISH!

EMMA L. BROCK

NEW YORK: *Alfred · A · Knopf*

Back-along in the good old days, there were four Cornish fishermen. They lived in Cornwall as Cornish people do. And they fished for fish.

Johnny was a little one no bigger than this. Dic and Willy were middle-sized. But Jan was as big and broad as all outdoors.

One day they scrubbed their boat. The *Bonnie Lass* she was and as blue as the Cornish sky. They stowed away their nets in the net room. The nets were black as a deep black Cornish night. They brought on board their bread and tea. And they were ready to fish for fish.

The sun was dropping to the sea as it does do every day. The motor of the *Bonnie Lass* began to chug. The *Bonnie Lass* slid out from Mousehole Town, chuggety, chug, chug. The *Bonnie Lass* ran out to sea. Chug, chug, chuggety, chug, chug.

The sun went down and evening came. Jan stood behind the wheel. He was steering by the compass there. Johnny lit the light on top the mast. Dic and Willy turned on the red and green ones on the left and right.

The *Bonnie Lass* sailed on-along twinkling her lights. She sailed on-along into the night to the fishing place to catch the fish. And there the four Cornish fishermen dropped the anchor overboard. The boat stood still, rocking on the waves.

"And now the nets," Jan shouted. "We'll shoot out the nets!" he cried. And that they did.

One by one, hand over hand, they shot out the nets. One, two, three, four, five, six, and more, each one fastened to the ones next to it. The last net was tied tightly to the *Bonnie Lass*. A mile of nets there was. The round canvas floats to hold the nets in place rode the sea like little ships. The black nets swung down into the sea and hung there. To catch the fish.

"There!" cried the four Cornish fishermen. "The pilchards will come down-along from the North Seas. The fish will tangle in the nets. More fishes for us! Come on-along, fish!"

And they hallooed and sang. Johnny in his little voice. Dic and Willy in their middle-sized

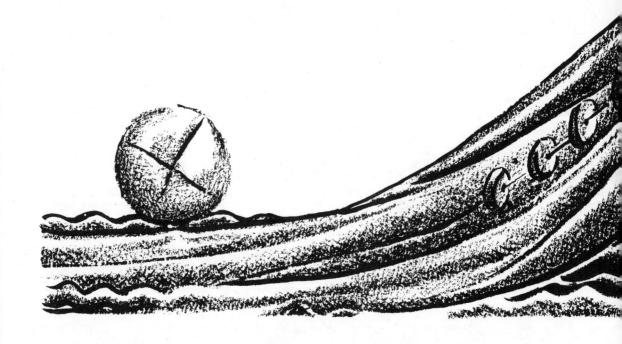

ones. And Jan in his big boom that rocked the sky around.

Then they had their tea down in the warm and tiny cabin. They boiled the water in the copper kettle and drank the tea from their blue mugs. They had bread, no butter. And Cornish ginger fairings their wives had made for them. Then they fell asleep on the locker seats. And dreamed of black nets filled with silver fishes. Their grins ran across their faces. Come on-along, fish!

But the wind came up, it did. It came up blowing from the west. It howled and blew, it did. It rocked the boat. It rocked the *Bonnie Lass* up and down. This way and that. She plunged and staggered.

The four Cornish fishermen rolled off their

locker seats. And they waked up wide awake.

"Agh!" yelled Jan. "The nets! It's blowing up a storm, that 'tis!"

They pulled on their high sea boots, did Jan, Will, Dic, and Johnny. They jerked on their

yellow slickers. They jammed their yellow storm hats down above their eyes.

"The nets!" they shouted and thumped up the stairs and out into the gale.

The wind came howling from the west.

"Whe-e-e-w," it blew. "Who-o-o-oh!"

It slapped their yellow slickers about their legs. It took the breath out of their mouths and blew it far over the sea. Jan and Will and Dic and Johnny held to the mast and to each other.

The rain was dashing down and the spray was whiffling up. And, ooh, a night it was as ever a night was! The black nets were pulling on the *Bonnie Lass.* They tipped her sideways in the waves. Pull, jerk, jerk!

"The nets!" Jan shouted. "We must save the nets!"

So they began to pull, did Jan, Will, Dic, and Johnny. They pulled. They hauled. They fought the waves. Slowly the nets began to move. Hand over hand they pulled them in. Johnny with his little pull no bigger than this. Dic and Willy with their middle-sized pulls.

And Jan with his big pull almost as strong as the waves.

But the sea jumped up. The *Bonnie Lass* slid down. The sea jumped up. The *Bonnie Lass* slid down to the bottom of the waves. And after her she dragged the black black nets that caught the fish.

Jan, Willy, Dic, and Johnny hauled the nets slowly from the black waters. How they did pull and how the waves pulled back at them!

Pull, pull, pull!

And, whoo, that wind did blow!

"Whe-e-e-e-w!" it blew. "Who-o-o-o-oh!"

It tore the nets from the cold fingers of Jan, Dic, Will, and Johnny.

"Hagh!" roared Jan. "Grab them!" he shouted, "or they'll be back in the sea again!"

They hauled, they groaned, they hauled again. Johnny pulled so hard that he fell flat with his sea boots in the air.

"Ugh!" he said.

Then Dic fell down with black nets around his neck.

"Ugh!" he grunted.

And Willy fell down too.

But big huge Jan pulled on. He pulled on alone. He puffed and panted, that he did. Jan and the nets pulled wildly at each other.

And how the wind did blow. It shook the *Bonnie Lass* from bow to stern. It shook her up and down and round about.

Jan pulled on the nets. The nets pulled back on Jan. Then Willy, Dic, and Johnny began pulling on them too. But the nets pulled harder. How those nets did pull! They pulled harder than all four of them together.

The *Bonnie Lass* stood up on edge. The black sea water swept up over the deck. And the four Cornish fishermen slid into the scupper.

"A knife!" yelled Jan. "We'll cut them loose. Or all of us and the boat too will be at the bottom of the sea!"

So with a big slice, slatch, Jan cut the ropes. He cut the ropes that tied two of the nets together. He sliced them through to the last thread of them. The untied nets slipped back into the blackness of the storm.

The *Bonnie Lass* tossed on through the tumbling rollers. She reared and plunged in the crashing water.

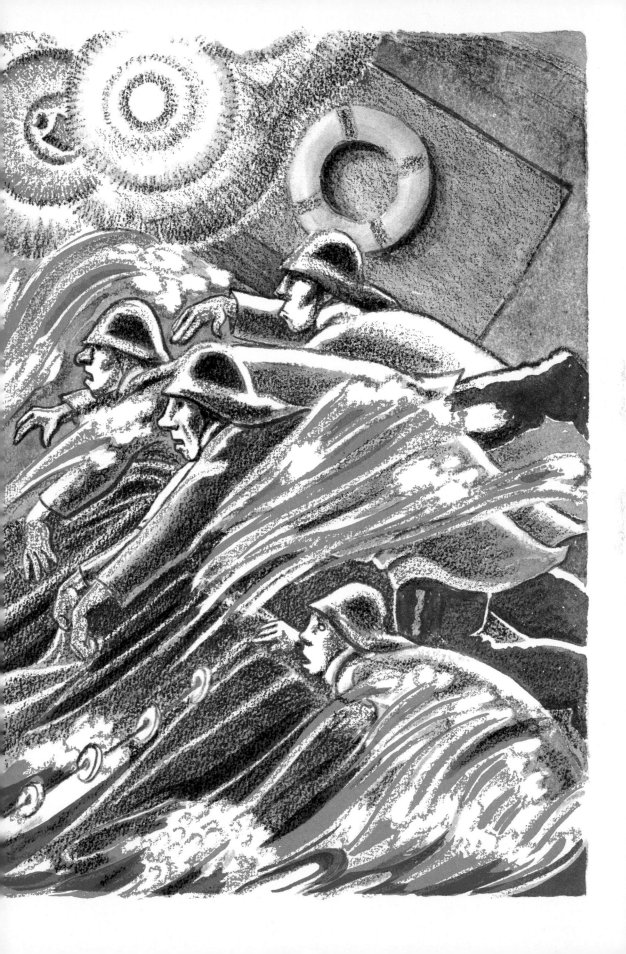

Jan, Willy, Dic, and Johnny dropped down on the pile of nets that they had saved. They gasped for breath. The rain and spray dashed over them. They rubbed their wet cold hands over their wet cold faces.

"The half of our good nets are gone!" moaned Jan. "And where be the money to buy new ones?"

"Ais!" said Dic and Willy.

"Ais!" said Johnny in a whisper.

"They be all gone!" they said sadly. "Gone!"

Oooo! What a storm as never a storm was!

But after an hour or so the wind died down. The storm blew on-along out toward the east. The *Bonnie Lass* rolled in the waves from side to side. But the gale was over and the morning came. The sun rose up and shone again.

Jan was in the wheelhouse. He was steering by the compass there. Johnny, Dic, and Willy were clumping about the deck in their big sea boots. They pulled at the tangled nets to straighten them. And they took out the silver pilchards that were caught in them.

The *Bonnie Lass* ran through the sea and into the port to the fish market there. They took off their yellow slickers, the four fishermen did. And hung them up to dry. They carried the pilchards to the market. All the fish they had, only half a catchful.

"Halloo!" called someone. "Halloo, there, Jan."

"Halloo," grinned Jan.

"Be it you lost some nets in the storm, Jan?"

"Why, ais. That's so," growled Jan. "The half and more! I cut them loose to save the boat."

"Ha!" grinned the other fisherman. "This morning at sunup what do we see?"

"What?" piped Johnny.

"Ha!" the fisherman said. "A string of floats and black nets be a-riding on-along all by themselves. We fetched them in. *Bonnie Lass* the floats said on them!"

"No!" Jan shouted. "Our nets!"

"Hurrah!" yelled Willy, Dic, and Johnny. "Our nets are back! Our nets have come home-

along again. Hurrah!" Jan in his big boom. Dic
and Willy in their middle-sized yells. And
Johnny in his little shout no louder than this.
"Hurrah! More fishes for us!"

Jan and Dic and Will and Johnny thanked
the other fishermen. They shook their hands
and slapped their backs. So glad were they that
the fishermen had brought their good black fishing nets home-along to them.

And they chuggety-chugged back to Mousehole Town. They hung the black nets, all the

black nets, a mile of them, on the wall to dry.
They sloshed down their boat to wash it clean.

Then with grins across their faces, up-along
the hill they thumped in their big sea boots.

Up-along the hill to Duck Street where their
families lived. And there they ate their hot beef-
and-'tater pasties and thick Cornish cream.

Johnny ate his little pasty no bigger than this.
Dic and Willy ate their middle-sized pasties.

And Jan ate his huge big pasty that was half the
size of all the land of Cornwall.

Between their bites of pasty, their mouths
grinned to their ears. Their nets were safe!
Come on-along, fish!

And the four Cornish fishermen lived happily ever after, fishing for fish. That they did!

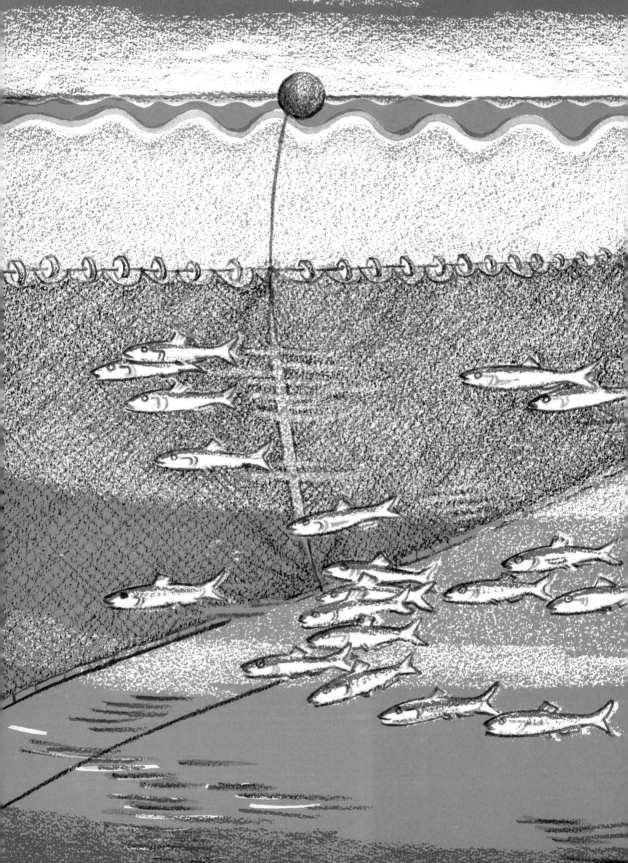